Ooo Shiny!
Volume 2
Holiday Edition 1

J M Samland

Copyright © 2023 by Jamie M Samland

Mary,
Making new friends in my 40s is hard enough, much
less one as objectively awesome as you. Thank you for
your unwavering support and nail polish.

Thanks

No book is written by a single person. Even a little thing like this is a product of many. Maybe I started a story as part of a prompt while at Panera with Mary, Elizabeth, Sarah, and Rob. Perhaps I saw something on a car ride with Aaron and it turned into something ridiculous that you'll soon be reading. My coworkers maintain an environment that is just below the stress level that would result in me becoming an alcoholic, allowing me to write at night. It could just be someone commenting that they're interested to know that I'm still doing this after three years.

So, a big thanks to my friends, family, cats, acquaintances, craft show neighbors, social media followers, and mailing list subscribers.

Thank you, Cabot. You're no Ash, but it was lovely always having your butt on my mouse pad as I wrote this. Though, and I know I ask you this often, why are you so bitey?

Another big thanks to my beta readers – Monidipa Dutta, Stephen Patten, Jennifer Poore, and Sarah Krzyzanski.

De Stahries

Wussis?

Well, here we are again. More little stories about nothing. This is my chance to ramble for a moment about whatever the heck I want to. It's my book. I do what I want. In my bit at the front of volume one, I briefly talked about where these stories came from: cemeteries and the IKEA catalog. What's next to chat about... How about what those stories mean to me?

I meet with a group of writer friends regularly at Panera or a local coffee place. After ninety minutes of chatting and catching each other up on the progress of our projects, one of us will sigh and say, "Well, should we write something?" We all grumble and take out our laptops. We decide on a writing prompt, set a timer (if we remember), and hit the keys for ten minutes. For me, one prompt turned into a story about a polite robot controlling a horde of dragons descending on New York City. For another in the group, it turned into a full romance novel. This is the core of writing, art, and expression. Two people look at the same thing and see it differently.

It's not that comic about two people staring at a number written on the ground between them. One sees "6," and the other sees "9". That's stupid, and it annoys me every time I see it posted. Someone wrote that number with the intention of it being read from one direction. If I hold a book upside down and read it all backward, no one is obligated to accept my viewpoint of a backward book as valid. It... Wait, what was I saying... What do these stories mean...

Individually, they're fun.

Collectively, they represent the unpredictability of the human brain. I'm not sure why I need to clarify "human" brain, as no other species are currently producing fiction, but I would absolutely buy a book written by a dolphin. I guess AI is coming up shockingly quickly, but screw that. Go away, AI.

The prompt is: "Write about a kid with a Christmas wish."

One writer creates a gritty world where a child wishes his parents would stop fighting.

Another writes an uplifting coming of age tale where a child wants a bike so they can avoid the bullies on the bus.

For me, a child creates a looping 43 minute hell and traps his family in it for eternity.

Same input, wildly different output.

This is the center of creative expression. We all look at the same sunset and each focus on something a little different in it. Then the means we use to express ourselves about it will all be different, too. There are eight billion of us alive right now and one source estimates something like 117 billion since our species became distinct 190,000 years ago. While the first few million probably weren't too complex by today's standards, imagine how you act and react differently than any others.

So while my rambling might start to come off like, "Everybody's so creative! Look how creative I, in particular, am about to be in this book!" that's not my intention. Short stories are one of my expressions, but everyone has their own, unique self. That's pretty cool.

Jan 1

This story is intended to be read out loud to someone else. Afterward, Google "squonk."

***

Holy crap, have I got a story for you! Okay, you know how we've been saying for a while that we need to get back to the gym? Well, not *need*, but *want*. I get enough exercise at work, and I know you do too, but there's something to be said about the routine of the gym. So, I've been watching them build that new FitHub247 by my work, the one that took over where the Cineplex7 closed last summer. Not that it really surprised me that the Cineplex closed. Their popcorn was too greasy and that's really the only reason I go to the movies anymore, for the popcorn. That and they didn't have an app for buying tickets. Or I guess they did, but it was just for Cineplex theaters and really janky and I'm not installing yet another janky app that wants a million permissions for something I'd use once, maybe twice, a month.

So anyway, they had their big grand opening — the gym, not the Cineplex, obviously — but I kept putting it off. Well, I finally went in the other night, but I put it off too long and missed their opening sales. The monthly fee's the same, I just missed out on the free duffle bag. That's fine. I have enough duffle bags. Though, yeah, can you really ever have too many duffle bags? As long as there's a place to store them all. That's a weird word, duffle. They were probably invented by Sir Francis Dufflesmyth, right?

Anyway, I went in after work the other day, so it was four in the morning. That would be my normal time going, so I wanted to see how busy it would be. Yeah, the parking lot was dead. I thought this'll be great. Get my reps in without anyone silently judging me. Like, even if literally no one ever looks in my general direction at the gym, I always feel like someone's breathing down my neck when I have to reduce the weight after seeing some old lady use the machine before me.

So anyway, the girl working had a big, gold septum ring. Not as big as that guy we saw at the L.A. Bookfest last year, but big and shiny. I'd never be able to get one of those. My allergies are too much and I have to blow my nose five times a day on a good day, to have something sticking in my nose all the time. I don't know how they can stand it. Maybe I'll ask her next time I see her. Though, how do you ask that without sounding like a creep? "Hey, how do you breathe with that thing in your nose?" Yeah, no.

Well, she's super nice and talks me through the amenities and different membership levels. I got the top level that lets me bring a guest, so if you want to hit the gym, let me know! The tanning and red light therapy rooms are only for members though, sorry. She's going on and on about all the machines and I'm all, "Yeah, get to the point!" I didn't say that, just thought it. She finally gives me a temporary pass and offers me the tour, but she's really stressing about how this gym is a "judgementless arena." Like, there's signs all over, so it was weird she kept saying it to me. Part of me was wondering if she was saying it for my benefit, which only made me more aware of my love handles and flat ass. Right before she opened the main door into the gym, she stopped again and says, "If this is when you'll be coming in, be extra aware of the policy," and she points to the "Judgmentless Arena" sign on the door.

Well, now I'm getting nervous, thinking they have, like, last season's cast of "30 Stone and Counting" back there. I nodded, she opens the door, and I hear the whir of treadmills.

The first person I saw was a big guy wearing an old FitHub247 tee. I never knew the gym etiquette. Do you grin and nod, or just ignore other people's existence there? But oh, when I turned the corner and saw who was on the far treadmill... The girl was going on with her tour, waving at the sections of the gym. Sandy, I think that was her name. That sounds right. She's going on about the weights and the circuit track. No, Cindy. Yes, Cindy. She walks me toward the back, toward the locker rooms, but all I can stare at is the other... I use the term "person" loosely here. I'm not being terrible, it genuinely wasn't human. And not in a "billionaires have dehumanized themselves with their complete lack of empathy for the working class" sort of inhuman, I mean it wasn't a homo sapien. Imagine if a pig, bear, elephant, and bloodhound all had a baby and got all the weirdest things from each. It's slowly stomping forward on the treadmill, skin all loose like it lost two hundred pounds overnight, dragging its feet. It had in headphones and was crying. Like, ugly crying. Tears streaking down its face, making the tread wet. I immediately thought it was listening to Taylor Swift or Sarah McLachlan, but again, no judgment. When we got close, I forced a grin and nodded. It looked up at me, gasped and...

It freaking exploded.

Poof! Into a cloud of mist, old sweats, and earbuds.

Like, what do you do when a person-ish thing explodes right in front of you? I just about fainted, but Sandy just took a deep breath. I'm trying to apologize, saying I wasn't judging, but knowing that I was a little inside, but she's all, "It's okay, this wasn't the first time. They'll be fine in a few hours," as she's turning off the treadmill. Cindy, rather. Not Sandy.

They freaking exploded!

I was like... What? Crazy, right?

I actually have seen them at the gym again since, but I never make eye contact. Like, I want to go up and apologize, but I bet it'll happen again. It's like a literal white elephant, except they're a bloodhound-pig-bear-thing.

So, long story short, if you want to go to the gym with me, let me know, but also, like, be very aware not to look around there.

Melted, Smooshed, and Snapped

The GPS tells me my destination's on the right, and I pull up in front of the ranch with a picket fence. I look over the blooming hydrangeas and mulched beds of lilies with a smirk and pick up the yellow piece of paper on the passenger seat.

"Wanted: Babysitter. Must be comfortable with dragon hatchlings and goblins. Must be able to defeat heroes. Pay 100 gold/hour. Text number below."

I'd taken the whole sheet rather than pull a tab with the phone number. A hundred gold an hour is almost twice what I made in any other gig, so this is either a joke or a very real and lucrative job offer. Besides, everyone knows goblins aren't real, and no one's seen a hero in decades. I'd texted the number and was told to be here at 7. I look down at my phone. I'm six minutes early.

I approach the door, staying on the neat trail of flat rocks through the front yard. A breeze catches the fresh lilacs, and I breathe them in with a smile as I ring the bell.

A balding, bespectacled man in a waistcoat and holding a pipe opens the door almost immediately.

"You must be Blenda," he says, sounding like his mouth is full of marbles, and steps back for me to enter. "I'm Domber. We spoke through text. Please, make yourself at home."

I enter the small mud room with a smile. As he shuts the door, the image of the staircase to the second floor and dated living room to the right dissolves into a stone cavern lit at the edges with torches and a larger fire in the center. A half dozen hallways snake away from the main chamber. Mr. Domber shakes off his illusion and rolls back his red-scaled shoulders. His glasses and pipe remain. I do the same to revert to my iridescent green scales.

Mr. Domber waves for me to follow him to the cavern's center while he talks. "Silid and Freeglyde are already asleep." He gestures down one path twisting away, then to another. "The clutch is safe with the hoard, and we ask you to leave them be."

A second red dragon strolls from the path leading toward the sleeping hatchlings.

"This is my mate, Vivordre," says Mr. Domber.

The other red dragon inclines her head slightly.

"We'll be back before moonset. You have my number if there are any problems," says Mr. Domber. "Any questions?"

A question about goblins and heroes sits at the edge of my tongue, but I bite it back with a wide smile. "No questions, Mr. Domber. You two have a fantastic evening. Happy Valentine's Day!"

Vivordre eyes me with the ghost of a sneer but says nothing as she follows Mr. Domber to the main cavern entrance.

I hear the door click closed, and the quiet stillness of the cave surrounds me. The soft lick of torches. The gentle drip of distant water. The tickle of a breeze from some faraway outlet. Moonset is six hours from now. Six hundred gold will go a long way to paying off student loans and one day getting a cave like this for myself, rather than my terrible studio apartment with two terrible human roommates. Humans are the worst; they smell so bad and are so short.

I debate going down the hall to check on the sleeping hatchlings but don't want to risk waking them. If they stayed asleep, it only made my job easier. Instead, I take a book from the case by the central brazier and curl up on the huge, round sofa.

A few pages into the trashy human romance novel, I hear a soft, quick pattering sound, like tiny feet slapping on the stone floor. I jerk up and search the corners of the cavern, first thinking the hatchlings are up. When the sound doesn't repeat, I settle back into the couch.

Something jumps onto my tail, and I surge backward with a yelp.

A small, dark green creature wearing a rusty iron skull-cap and nothing else stands on the couch, grinning at me with a gap-toothed smile. When my wits return, I recognize the beast from old academic drawings.

"A goblin?" I move closer to squint at the little thing.

It coos and squints back at me. It's ugly, but in a cute way, and seems harmless enough. I settle back into the couch, and it flops down against my tail. It gets less cute as it starts licking itself. Within a minute, it seems to have forgotten about me as it's fully engrossed in grooming itself against my tail. The rhythm of its aggressive cleaning almost lulls me to sleep, but something pokes at the edges of my hearing again. It grows nearer until I can identify it: Human speech.

Goblins and possible heroes all in one night? Is Mr. Domber and Vivordre's cave cloaked not only within a suburban community but also displaced in time?

The goblin hisses when I shoo it off me, but it scampers down the hall toward the hatchlings' room, its skullcap bouncing on its head as its feet slap the stone.

I shrink and contort to my human form before hiding in the shadows. The voices grow nearer, at least five of them.

"Keep your wits about you, lads," says one in a haughty tone. "Let my shield protect us from the vile fire-breathing wyrm's flames."

"Actually," says another, "it would be a fire-exhaling wyrm."

"Shut up, Droderick," chorus no fewer than three.

Torchlight flickers into view down one of the corridors, and I move closer before a human in brilliant silver armor with a tower shield in one arm and a massive hammer over the other shoulder struts forward. "The wyrm's lair!" he announces while the others try to quiet him.

Please do, I think. *Don't wake the hatchlings!*

Five in total. Two in cloth robes, two in leathers, one with a long bow strapped across her back.

One wearing cloth and a tall hat blinks, and his eyes glow with an inner light. He speaks in a whispered lisp. "This cavern doth sparkle with the intricacies of magic. I will prepare us a portal for which to escape with our treasures, forthwith."

I watch him wave his hands while the others slowly spread out across the chamber. The archer takes her long bow, an archaic weapon with no place indoors, in one hand and an arrow in the other. "Yar," she growls, "I smell the stink of a dragon bitch. There'll be eggs with the hoard." She smacks her lips. "Delicious eggs."

The other wearing cloth robes waves a golden holy symbol on a chain. "Ulnir tells me more treasure lay down this path." He gestures toward where the goblin had scurried, toward the sleeping hatchlings.

I snarl and step into the light. "Hey."

Weapons and attention snap toward me.

"A blood witch!" cries the wizard.

I look down at my purple wool sweater, yoga pants, and Crocs and back up at them with a curse on my lips. I should have put on an illusion of more appropriate clothing.

"No, not a witch," I say in the human tongue. "The dragons that live here had me captive but, yea! You saved me! Let's go. They'll be back any moment." I wave them toward the path they'd entered from, much like I'd shooed the goblin.

"Go, fair non-witch," says the priest. "I will smite the foul wyrms where they rest, in Ulnir's name!" He steps toward the hatchling's hallway, and I jump to bar his way.

"No, nothing down there. Believe me; I've been their prisoner for months."

I see the last of their party in dark leathers that had yet to speak sneaking through the shadows on the far side of the room toward the hoard and clutch of eggs. I can't protect both sides at once unless...

The priest flies back as I snap a shining green wing into his chest. The rogue leaps away, narrowly dodging the line of acid I belch at him. It hisses on the stone just inches from his boots. The wizard produces a staff from his robes to chant a ritual spell.

"A viridian poison dragon!" the priest shouts as he pushes to his feet, raising his holy symbol toward me. "In Ulnir's name! Smite this foul—" His words cut off in a gurgling scream as my acid melts him to a puddle. Holy symbol and all.

The warrior in gleaming armor is upon me a second later, swinging his comically unwieldy hammer in slow arcs that I easily avoid. The rogue thinks he's sneaky, but I flick my tail, sending him sailing through the cave to slide down a far wall with a crunch. Pain blossoms in my right shoulder, and I look down at the satisfied smirk from the archer with the long bow. The warrior exclaims his triumph as he hits me in the flank while I slither to snap the bow in half. I savor the archer's empty-handed terror for half a breath before I also snap her.

The warrior hits me again in the ribs and I groan with the pain. That will leave a bruise. Whirling back on him with tooth and wing, I drive the armored man back toward the entrance, stepping on the chanting wizard by accident as I did. The warrior blocks attack after attack with his tower shield until I grab it in my fangs and toss it away. His arm flops worthless at his side, broken or dislocated from my wrenching, and he swings wildly with his hammer. I evade or deflect the blows as they come while wondering what Mr. Domber and Vivordre would have me do with heroes. Should I kill them all? Others might come to rescue this lot. Let one flee as a warning? Others would come to prove their might. There's no winning solution.

As my mother would say, I have to make an executive decision. I stop toying with the warrior and cough a splotch of acid across his gleaming armor. His screams echo behind me, hopefully not loud enough to wake the hatchlings, and I turn to scour for where the rogue had landed. I spot him limping toward the horde hallway and rush to finish him with another snap of my muzzle.

I tidy the melted, smooshed, and snapped remains of the heroes into a neat pile by the entrance, leaving them for Mr. Domber to deal with when they returns. I curl up back on the wide couch and try to remember what was happening in the trashy human romance novel just as the hatchlings start to cry.

The hundred gold an hour feels a little less like easy money as I shoo the goblin off me and get up to see to hatchlings.

2nd of Vylilt

"Dear Sir, you are hereby notified that you were, on the 37th day of Tleulp, 435, legally drafted in the services of the Seelie Court in accordance with'..." Ted stared at the paper with a very official-looking letterhead featuring an ornate throne wrapped in curling vines. He handed it back to Mika. "What is this?"

Mika flipped over the envelope the letter had come in. "Ser Corgnealius" was written across the front in a sweeping, looping script, but no house address. "Something for Corgs." He looked down at their Welsh corgi sitting between them on the kitchen floor, tongue lolled, waiting for second dinner.

"Yeah, but, what? Drafting the dog into a faerie army? Is it a marketing gimmick for a new groomer?"

Mika turned over the page and shrugged, dropping both it and the envelope on the island. "It doesn't have an address, just says to be ready on the second of Vylilt, because, you know, that means something."

Ted took the paper, ripped it in half, and dropped it into the recycling bin. "I just feel old, not understanding how they think this will work." He tapped his thigh as he walked from the room. "Come on, Ser, time for sleepies."

Ser Corgnealius gave up his vigil for food and followed his dads to bed.

Ted woke moments before his alarm to an empty bed. He found Mika in the kitchen, leaning over the island with a crisply creased piece of paper unfolded in his hands. "What's that?" He poured himself a cup of coffee and leaned over Mika to read. He instantly recognized the letterhead and jumped back. "I tore that up."

Mika looked up with wide eyes and an ashen pallor. "There was another right here." He tapped a finger on the kitchen island in front of him.

Ted choked on his coffee. "Someone was in the house?"

Mika opened his mouth to respond but only blew out a long, shaky breath. The letter fell from his fingers.

"This is your sister being a shit, right? She's mad we didn't go to her poetry reading last month and she's... I don't know what."

"This one's dated the first of Vylilt. If tomorrow will be the second, that's when it says Corgs is being drafted."

Mika looked down at the corgi sitting at his feet, tongue lolled, waiting for breakfast. "Do we go to the cops?"

"And say faeries are delivering letters to us in the night? When we called them about Stan and Janice shooting bottle rockets at our house, they didn't give a shit as soon as they saw it was two guys. You think they'll do anything?"

Mika flicked the letter across the island and ran a hand through his hair. "This is stupid." He chuckled dryly and rubbed his face. "Some stupid prank, but I don't get it. Who's doing it and why? We have to get out of here. I don't like the idea of things just showing up in the house. Let's... let's go to your mom's for the weekend."

Ted leaned back against the counter and considered his husband for a long moment before pushing off with a nod. "Sure, yeah. We'll leave right now. I just need to email work and text mom we're coming."

They had little to say on the drive from the suburbs and through cornfields and rural towns. Ser Corgnealius' contented panting from Mika's lap added to the monotony of road noise and more corn. He switched to an excited whine when they pulled into the gravel driveway of the lake house that had been Ted's childhood home.

"My favorite sons!" Jillian yelled from the front door and came to greet them. Ted's mom rushed to dole out hugs, kisses, and promises of homemade brownies. "I was about to call you this morning right before I got your text, Teddy. I've been getting the weirdest stuff in the mail lately."

"What was it?" Ted asked.

"Come in and put your stuff down, and I'll show you."

Mika shot Ted a wide-eyed glance as he shouldered their bags. Ser Corgnealius ran ahead and through the front door.

"What's it called?" Jillian said over her shoulder, following the dog. "Viral marketing or something? I don't get it. Just tell me what you're selling and get it over with."

Ted and Mika hastened their pace, running past Jillian and into the house.

"Where's the letter?" Ted crossed the shag carpet of the living room, reflexively greeted the long-haired orange tabby on the piano bench with a "Hey, Marms," and stepped into the lime linoleum of a kitchen lifted directly from a decor era few hoped would make a resurgence. He snatched up the tri-folded page from the table, fingers trembling when he saw the familiar format of the letter, and scanned the words.

Still holding their day bags, Mika read over his shoulder. "The letterhead is different," he commented, tracing the crown and vines with a finger. "It's drafting Marmalade to the Unseelie Court, due on the second of Vylilt." He glanced back at the cat in the living room. Marmalade stood, stretched, and hopped from the piano bench to saunter out of sight.

Jillian passed the cat and entered the kitchen. "What do you boys think? I got one of those in the mail daily for the last week and I keep throwing them out. Someone has too much free time on their hands."

Ted and Mika could only stare at each other, unable to form a phrase or single word to express their confusion and mounting dread. Mika's glance strayed to the envelope on the table with Marmalade's name written in a sweeping, looping script. Something lay beneath it. He pushed Marmalade's envelope aside. Mika stumbled back and into a chair.

"What is it?" Jillian stepped between them and frowned down at the table. "Did you boys bring that in?"

Ted swallowed hard and stared down at "Ser Corgnealius" written in that now-familiar script.

***

I love these guys so much—just the idea of a mid-30s couple trying to live their lives, but boom, fae. I offer this story free through my mailing list, but I couldn't resist including it here. I fully intend for this story's expansion to be my next novel. They won't hesitate for a breath to rush into the fae lands and save Ser Corgnealius, but once they're there, would they want to return?

The Christmas Miracle

Zack woke with the creaking of his bedroom door but feigned slumber as his daughters crept up on him. He wanted to cry out with the agony of his frayed mind even as the girls jumped.

"Daddy! Daddy! Get up! It's Christmas!"

He laughed and tickled but couldn't unsee the same torment in their eyes, hidden deep behind the giggles and flailing arms. Despite their rosy cheeks and dimples, their eyes pleaded for something denied to them all.

"Where's your brother?" He asked and stepped into his slippers. The girls jumped on the bed.

"He's downstairs. Said he couldn't wait," said Grace between hops.

Zack knew what would happen next but still felt the surge of adrenaline when she stumbled and fell, bumping her head on the footboard. He gathered her up, checked for bleeding while she wailed, kissed and rocked her, and cooed her name, saying she'd be fine. Of course, she would be. She always was. Her older sister sat frozen, but her eyes looked bored.

Zack carried Grace to the kitchen, and she declared she was fine by the time the first Pop-Tarts were ready. He mechanically swept crumbs into his palm and brushed them in the sink.

"Food time, Nick," he called. "Food first, then we'll open presents."

Nick entered a moment later, dragging his stuffed cephalopod behind him. He wiped his bleary eyes and pulled himself onto the stool between his sisters.

Zack lay across the kitchen island closer to his three beautiful children. He tapped the end of his older daughter's nose with a "boop." The four laughed at his terrible dad jokes that might have been funny the first few times, but he'd stop counting at a hundred. That was an eternity ago. An eternity of torment he could see his children shared by the hollow void of their eyes, but were powerless to escape.

"Are you excited for Christmas, buddy?" he asked his son.

"Yeah! I love Christmas," Nick answered with a gap-toothed lisp, picking at the remains of his Pop-Tart. Zack and the girls focused on him with grins that didn't reach their eyes.

Zack tousled his boy's messy hair and pushed back to pour himself a mug of coffee as the machine beeped. "Let's see what Santa brought." He followed his children as they ran to the living room. Through the picture window facing the drive, he waved at the neighbors shoveling their sidewalk across the street. They waved back. Zack had no recollection of their names or what history they shared. Were they real and trapped in the same hellish torment as he and his kids? Or did they move on to experience their lives, oblivious to their neighbor's suffering?

Nor did Zack remember his own life outside of his children. What did he do for a living? Who was the president? Where was their mother? Dead? Divorced? Away on business? Zack didn't wear a wedding band, but that meant little. He had no idea of his older daughter's name because no one had said it. He only knew his own because "Zack's" was printed in festive holiday print on his coffee mug. Maybe Zack was his husband.

Zack turned and sat beside the tree as Nick tore open a wrapped cephalopod to match his other.

The boy gasped and squealed with delight, hugging the squid and octopus tightly. "I love it! I wish Christmas never ended!"

Zack's vision blurred to black. He long ago gave up on trying to scream his rage.

Zack woke with the creaking of his bedroom door, but feigned slumber as his daughters crept up on him.

Jean and Jace

"**W**e're running out of time.'"

"Shut up, Mike," Linda groaned and adjusted the thick collar of her bomb disposal suit.

"I'd say that's famous last words, but I don't know if anyone heard them." Mike stood on his toes to see the long line dwindling to a speck in front of the pair, to the limitless white that was the group, horizon, and sky. He turned to the line behind them just as long.

"Our radios were open. Someone heard it."

Mike shifted the weight between his feet and looked down at the fluffy white wisps billowing around his shins. "What's taking so long?"

"It's the gates of heaven. Of course there's a line," Linda said with an eye-roll behind her face shield. "I'm sure the rate of deaths is a lot higher now than when it was built. Think of how much I-696 gets backed up at rush hour. Except it's always rush hour."

"I didn't realize you were such an expert in the afterlife."

"I've thought about it often in our line of work."

"So what went wrong?" Mike asked. "We traced the circuit, eliminated the false ones. I'd stake…" He paused with a chuckle. "I was about to say I'd stake my life on being right. You know what I mean."

The pair shuffled forward to close the gap in front of them.

Linda shrugged, her heavy suit barely moving with the motion. "Maybe the timer was counting down to ninety seconds. Maybe there was another device. Maybe a meteor landed on us. Maybe we can ask when we get to the front of the line. Maybe we'll never know."

They shuffled forward again.

"At least we're moving," said Mike and craned his neck to catch the first glint of light off the distant pearly silver. "Ever wonder why heaven has gates? Are they keeping something in? Or something out? Do gates mean there are defined borders?"

"It's all symbolism," said Linda. "We're limited mortals that can't truly comprehend the abstract. We have to label and categorize everything, know how it feels and tastes, how it reacts under an electrical current. We're just creating a visual representation of input our minds can't comprehend, seeing what we expect to see."

Mike scratched at the hood of his suit. "I'd expect this line would move faster."

They shuffled forward.

"I just realized…" Mike started. "We're dead. This sucks, but I expected to be more broken up about it. I just sort of feel hollow."

"I know, right?"

They kept pace in silence for a while before Mike broke it. "You really have thought about this a lot. We worked together for four years, and I don't really know you, Linda."

"That's intentional, Mike. Our job is nothing but stress, and I want nothing to do with it when I'm off the clock."

Mike grunted thoughtfully. "Makes sense. So now that it doesn't matter, tell me, who did you leave behind?"

"A wife, a hamster, a crippling mortgage."

"A wife? No shit." Mike repeated with a wide grin hidden behind his mask. "My boyfriend was about to move in. We've been together two years, but his cat hates my dog." He paused and let the conversation drift away. "I'm sad thinking about Jace, but it's more that I'm sad that I'm not sad. Being upset about the lack of something I know should be there." He paused and licked his dry lips. "Am I making any sense?"

"I didn't finish my novel," Linda whispered. "I worked on it every morning before Jean woke up. She didn't know about it, but I was going to give her the first draft on our tenth anniversary. Now when she gets the dump of my digital legacy cloud backups, she won't know to look for it."

They stepped forward.

"What's it about?" Mike asked.

"It's trash, just a gigantic pile of the worst tropes. A big city lawyer — Jean's an attorney — goes home to the ranch — like what I grew up on — for the holidays and falls for the lady shepherd her family hired. It's stupid, something that would be on an off-brand Hallmark station after midnight on a Tuesday."

"I mean, I don't know Jean at all, but that sounds like just about the most romantic thing someone could do; create something to symbolize your love."

Linda chuckled wryly and wiped pointlessly at her mask. "Thinking of that has me thinking about Jean. I'm finally starting to miss her, not just sad about the lack of sadness, like you said. Actually missing her."

The group in front of the pair shuffled closer, forcing Mike and Linda to retreat a step.

"Rude," Mike grumbled. He rubbed at a pain in his chest. Heartburn in heaven? Well, outside of heaven.

"How were you going to have Jace's cat and your dog get along?"

"I suggested we let them share a steak," said Mike. "Food is always the best unifier."

"Unless your dog runs off with it."

"Barkenstein is fifteen, toothless, and not stealing anyone's steak. He'd just lap the juices while Steve eats the actual meat and growls the whole time." He sighed.

"What?"

The group pressed at the pair again, and they stepped back.

"Thinking about Jace, I felt nothing. Now I'm on the verge of collapsing into a blubbery mess, thinking about what we won't have together like you and the book with Jean. Jace is an installation artist. He had cosmic-level plans for my loft apartment with all that exposed brick."

A stab of pain shot through Mike's chest, doubling him forward. Linda dropped to a knee in her bulky suit. The group before them pressed back, pushing the pair from the line that quickly closed up. The agony shot through him again, like his heart would explode from his chest. He struggled to breathe through burning lungs, though he couldn't remember needing air while standing in line. As he collapsed to his knees, then to his side, he faced the line of recently deceased that shrank and lost focus with each labored hammer of his heart. Mike struggled to turn toward the pearly gates once more, to catch a last view of the light glinting so far away.

A regular, high beep crept into Mike's mind, instantly recognizable as a heart rate monitor. He took a thin breath, cringing at the ache in his chest, but the tube across his nose helped to press oxygen into him. Mike struggled to open his mouth, which felt full of glue, and moaned instead.

He felt pressure on his right hand, a soft squeeze perhaps. Someone made gentle shushing sounds, and a plastic straw touched his lips. He sucked in the tepid water that burned all the way down to his stomach. Despite the discomfort, he drank more to unstick his mouth and form a single word.

"Linda?"

The silence lasted long enough that Mike was unsure he'd made any sound.

"She's alive," Jace whispered. "Focus on you right now."

Days passed until the bandages were removed to let Mike see the world again. The doctors told him the concussive force of the device stopped his heart for two full minutes. Other than burns and a pacemaker at twenty-nine, he was whole. Saved by the protective gear, Linda was as well off but had yet to wake.

Three weeks later, the doctors released him. Though he could walk, Jace wheeled him to the exit per hospital regulations. Mike stood and walked back in, aiming for the long-term care with Jace on his heels.

The ward held six beds. A woman with dark hair pulled back in a tie sat near the window, holding the hand of the room's only patient. She quickly snatched her hand back to her lap and looked at him with red-rimmed eyes that hadn't seen decent sleep in a month.

"It's okay, Jean," Mike said and started, unsure how he knew her name.

She relaxed and returned her hand to Linda's. "You must be Mike. Linda never told me much about you, but if you know of me, you know why."

"It's the weirdest thing," Mike said and sat on the edge of the nearest empty bed. He looked down at Linda, looking restful with a few light bruises on her cheek and a suture on her forehead. "I feel like she and I talked for hours on everything. I know all about you, your hamster, the summer cottage, her secret boo—" He caught himself quickly and raised his voice to cover it. "But I don't remember having the actual conversations. We must have talked while on the job, and the adrenaline did something to my memory. Getting blown up jostled it all to the front." Jace sat beside him and wrapped an arm around his waist.

Jean hid her face in her hands, sobbing quietly, and Mike realized the callousness of his words. "Shit, I'm sorry, Jean."

She snatched a tissue. "It's... The doctors aren't sure if she'll wake up. I know I shouldn't, but it's how my mind works. I'm already thinking of cleaning out our cottage up in St. Sorsha. Linda will need somewhere quieter to recover. I could sell it as-is, but need to get in that safe in the closet."

"The code's 12-34-5," said Mike without thinking.

Jean stared at him for a breath before cracking a grin. "The same combination on her luggage. She must have told you everything on the job."

"More than I realized. Hey, St. Sorsha's only about a two-hour drive, and you look like you could use the air. I'll stay with Linda."

Jace frowned, clearly wanting to go home.

"You sound like you know what's in that safe, Mike."

"Something Linda would want you to read."

"I could use the air." Jean gathered her bag and leaned to kiss Linda on the cheek. "I'll be back before the night nurse makes her rounds." She dabbed at her eyes and faced Mike. "Normally, impulsiveness like this isn't like me. I must really need to step out for a moment. That staff all has my number."

"What was that, babe?" asked Jace a moment after Jean was out of sight. "What's in that safe?"

"The book Linda was writing for Jean."

"How romantic. Wow, you two must have talked about everything on the job."

"We never talked," said Mike, looking down at Linda. "Yet I know everything about her."

A Fae at Heart

After two days of following every rabbit hole in every social media video sharing service, learning all I could about the origins of English, Middle-English, and the shared roots of Proto-Germanic, I went east. From another YouTube video came the syllables of Thai and Mandarin that my palate couldn't create and my ear couldn't discern. Maybe back west to the native Mayan languages. I spoke gibberish at my monitor, mashing together sounds and phrases that don't exist in my native tongue.

"Why is this so hard?" I leaned back and scratched fingers through my greasy hair. I should shower, but the first draft was so close to being done. A final note from my past self glared in white text against the dark-mode background.

<<say 'hi' in low-dwarven>>

I knew everything else about the low dwarves. How they dress, style their homes, and their monarch's complex family tree dating back a dozen generations. But how do they say hi? I wasn't creating a language with grammar and clauses, just a single word of greeting spoken when my reluctant protagonist first encounters his bearded, would-be girlfriend. The hundred-and-thirty-thousand-word novel was a tightly woven story of mystery, action, romance, and more twists than... something twisty. My best work yet. It would sell a million copies, and the streaming services would get into knife fights on my front lawn over who would buy the series rights.

But, as with any story, it hinged on that intriguing inciting incident. The first time the enemies-turned-lovers meet. It all depended on her lowering her double-headed battle ax and choosing diplomacy over violence. On her saying hello.

In low-dwarven.

Whatever that sounded like.

If I didn't know how she sounds, do I really know her? Are the tens of thousands of words that follow all a lie? Would I have to scrap it all when I decide the greeting changes her personality?

I twisted my cheeks and lips around the sounds. Were anyone looking in my sunroom window, they'd call the loony bin to collect me.

"Hey," said a small voice to my left.

I yelped and tipped sideways in my wicker chair, cracking my elbow on the tile floor. Pushing to my knees, I peered over the coffee table at the man standing beside my laptop. I use the term loosely, but his dark, three-piece tailored suit fit him perfectly down to polished leather shoes. Except he was only five or so inches tall. And had light purple skin. And wings like a monarch butterfly sprouted from the back of his coat.

"Sorry to startle you," he said in that same small voice. "Could you give me your name?"

"Dev," I answered automatically and crawled nearer to the table's edge.

The little purple man grinned, then frowned with a grunt. "What are you?"

"I could ask you the same." My eyes flicked to the two empty bottles of Jack beside my laptop. No, whiskey doesn't give hallucinations. Well, at least not store-bought stuff.

He shrugged, a tiny gesture. "Yeah, but I asked you first."

"I'm... I'm a writer." I eyed my phone beside the laptop and wondered if I could grab it to make a video recording of this. It would make a great short story later. No, this had to be a dream. A whiskey-fueled dream. In the waking world, my cheek was spamming pages of "sssssss."

"What are you?" I asked.

"*What* and not *who*?" he tsked and paced behind my laptop's screen. "Slightly rude, but I'll overlook it. Name's Lemony Muddybay, Second Emissary to the Queen's Court. I'm sorry. Could you give me your name again?"

"Dev," I repeated. "Dev Sheridan."

Lemony raised his eyebrows with a gasp and again frowned with a grunt.

"You're a fairy," I said.

He chuckled. "And you're a human! My people prefer being called fae. I'll let it slide, as you probably haven't met many of my kind before. Dev... Is that short for something?"

"It's what my Pa always called... Wait... Are you trying to steal my name? Isn't that what fairies, um, fae, do?"

Lemony leaned against my laptop's screen and stuck his fists against his hips. "So rude! You summon me here and then lay out all these slanderous, racist accusations about my ancestors?"

"I'm sorry, I..." I stammered and shook my head, sitting back on my heels. "Wait, I summoned you?"

"Yeah, imagine my surprise. I was putting my feet up with a nectarine beer after a long day when I got the call. I didn't think *you people* had any summoners left alive."

I thought of my attempts to create a greeting in low-dwarven and shook my head. The idea that I tapped into lost, ancient magics while stringing together awkward phonemes was... no... stupid...

"What, eh, what do we do now?" I asked.

Lemony shrugged again. "You're the one that called me here. What do *you* want?"

Despite everything about the situation, my mind cleared just enough. It probably assumed I could sort out the strangeness of talking to a five-inch fae later.

"Assume I don't know why most people might summon a fae," I said. "What are the options?"

"Nothing sexual." Lemony's tone was dark and absolute.

I winced back. "My god, of course not. Is... Has that happened?"

Lemony's frown broke into a wide grin. "The look on your face! Ha! But no, seriously." He craned his neck and took flight with a single flap of his wings. He turned a slow circle, his wings barely moving to keep him hovering in place. "Hmm, I sense nothing magical about you. Maybe you did summon me by accident. Very well, I can help a little, just nothing too dirty." He gestured at his pressed suit and polished shoes and lowered to stand again beside my laptop.

"I thought you were about to put your feet up. You relax wearing that?"

Lemony scoffed. "I'm fae, not a farmer. What were you working on when you accidentally ripped me from my home plane?"

"I was trying to sound out a word to make up for my book."

"You don't have enough words already that you need to make up new ones?"

"It's for a critical scene! The hero barely survives the battle and—"

"Yeah, yeah, don't care." Lemony kicked off my laptop screen and waved off my words. "So you were making up a word in a language that you'll use how many times in his story?"

"Once."

He raised an eyebrow.

"It's a critical scene." I frowned.

"Wouldn't you agree that creating a fragment of a language that you'll use exactly once is needlessly complex? Will reading your soup of letters and punctuation enhance the reader's experience?"

"Maybe, but I—"

"Maybe you nothing. As Second Emissary, I am fluent in over three hundred languages and can cast simple glamors to understand the rest. What language is this word spoken in?"

"Low dwarven."

Lemony's shoulders dropped, and he pinched the bridge of his nose. "Damned fantasy writers." He sucked in a deep breath and looked back at me. "I'll provide you with an English to Underdwarf dictionary in exchange for you casting the magics to return me home."

"I don't know how—"

"I'll write them down phonetically. Burn the paper afterward. Now, for the paperwork." Lemony pulled a notebook and tiny pen from the inner breast pocket of his coat. "Please give me your full legal name for the official records." He clicked the pen.

"Vinay Dev— Oh no! No, you don't, you sneaky thing."

Lemony huffed and scribbled something in his notebook. "Can't blame a fae for trying." He tore out the page before tucking away the notepad and pen.

He handed me the paper, and I accepted it on an index finger, raising my glasses to squint at the tiny letters. "It's too small," I said.

"Just try to read it. It's magic. Here's your thing."

I looked up at Lemony and the four-by-six-inch book sitting on the table beside him. As promised, "English to Underdwarf, Third Edition, Revised and updated with conversational phrases" was printed in yellow and red letters across the front.

"Read it," the fae said and pointed at my hand. "It's beer o'clock."

Looking back at his paper, the tiny runes swam in my mind as I focused on them. It was like trying to pronounce something written in Greek, with completely foreign letters, but somehow a sound came to my lips, gurgling awkwardly up from my throat. The page burst into flames, and I yelled, more from surprise than pain.

Lemony Muddybay was gone.

I snatched up the dictionary and finally righted my chair to sit in front of the laptop again. Thumbing through, I found the standard Underdwarf greeting and the approximated spelling using English characters. I tried to pronounce it, but the strings of consonants didn't flow smoothly. My fingers hovered over the keyboard, ready to type the fourteen letters that would complete my first draft.

They continued to hover.

No.

My hands dropped to my lap.

Lemony was right. This string looks like my mom's cat spelled it out. It would only pull the reader from the narrative and serve no real purpose.

My hands returned to the keys.

She lowered her ax and swept a hand through her beard. She uttered something I recognized as her native language; something scholars labored to decipher for decades across this bloody war. I might have beaten them to their task. She was saying hello to me.

I danced in my seat while I hit save a dozen times, exported the final first draft to back up across the cloud, and scrolled to the bottom to type a giant "THE END" before saving a screenshot to post on social media.

But a seed of doubt lingered within me. A seed that didn't exist twenty minutes ago. That critical scene required hearing the low-dwarven greeting because it wasn't just that she said hello but that she used the familiar form. It implied she saw something in the protagonist that stayed her blade. It created intrigue.

No, this isn't right.

I scrolled back up, rolling my eyes at "uttered something." What a cop-out.

Maybe this whole book is a contrived mess. Is there anything unique to the story or characters? The enemies-to-lovers subplot is clearly forced. Will anyone other than my mother even want to read it? Not with an inciting incident as terrible as this.

Thank you, Lemony Muddybay. I thought fae were supposed to be tricksy, but then, I didn't think they were real. I thought you gave me a single phrase of greeting, but you made me realize my last eight months were a waste.

The Zoo

"Three cilveads, four feesu, nineteen assaiths, twenty-four terrans, and thirty-two kurguls," Util read from the manifest that flashed across zis display.

"What's that last one?" Azoc asked, looking up from the work order on ters own display.

"Kurguls? These are rescued from the outpost—"

"No, sorry," Azoc interrupted, "the one before that. Terrans?"

"They're rare, the first ones here." Util tapped at zis display with a tentacle and a three dimension wireframe diagram formed in the space between the pair. It slowly rotated to show the species from every angle. "Bi-pedal omnivores from the third planet of the locally-called Sol system." Orange text flashed below the image, causing Util to grimace. "They're incredibly violent, requiring special care facilities."

"I sometimes wonder why we want to preserve every species," said Azoc, whistling through ters trunk. "Twelve breeding pairs. They breed in *pairs*? How boring. How can they ensure sufficient gene diversity?"

"They're not here for a breeding program, they're just packaged that way."

"It just seems strange and inefficient."

"The notes state they frequently go through bonding rituals outside their breeding pairs. Apparently, that leads to more intra-species fighting. This also says they need a lot of toys. The shinier, the better." Util shrugged, zis entire carapace lifting and dropping with the motion, and gestured at the spinning model. "Exterior reproductive organs. They really lost the evolutionary lottery. No wonder they're nearly extinct."

Azoc scanned the list in ters tentacle and made a low fluting sound. "Why am I not seeing terrans on the placement order? I see all the others."

Util turned back to zis display and tapped. "They're definitely on their way. Estimated arrival in seven half-lifes."

"*Seven*? I have no place to put these things and they'll be here before our next restoration period? Can we put them in with another exhibit for now?"

"Maybe with the cilveads?" Util offered. "They're similar sizes. Though, wait, what's the terran environment like?" Zie manipulated the screen and stared at the results.

"What? What is it?" Azoc asked after a moment of silence.

In response, Util pivoted the display.

"Oxygen?" Azoc staggered. "They breathe oxygen? No wonder they're so aggressive! They're fire breathers! There's no way I can get a habitat ready for them in time. They'll have to stay in their shipping crate until we're ready."

Potato Salad and the Lake House

Senior Detective McClacky shuffled through the stack of red folders, tossing them one at a time onto an uneven pile in front of him. What should have been a gentle last two weeks before retirement quickly morphed into one of the most gruesome cases of his long career. Each folder burst with paper-clipped crime scene photos with a clear pattern. There was another killer on the loose in this quiet vacation town. A killer that spared no one and left McClacky wondering how the victims could possibly contain so much blood. Yet after five crime scenes, they'd yet to find a scrap of evidence of the killer. Not a single fingerprint, shoe impression, hair, or clothing fiber. The local cops from this little rural town were starting to whisper of a murderous ghost. It was all McClacky could do to contain the story from the press without the added worry of the cops leaking paranormal hogwash.

The sleepy town of St. Sorcha was all locals and off-season renters right now, but another two weeks would bring thousands for the Off-Road Vehicles Fest, signaling the start of the "on season." If the killer wasn't caught by then, he would have a much easier time finding new targets in the noise and traffic.

Or she, McClacky thought. *Ladies can be mass murderers these days, too.*

He reached for the files again, but what would be the point? He'd been through them enough to commit every detail to memory. The victims had no connections. Nothing beyond residing in this little town. And with nothing in common, there was no way to predict who would be next.

"Hey, sir," said the impossibly young Junior Detective Miles Dunn. He didn't look old enough to drive, let alone solve crimes. "I'm heading to the Dollar Plus. You need anything?"

McClacky didn't, but neither did he need to keep sitting behind the desk doing nothing.

"I'm driving," he said, snatching his coat and hat from the back of the chair.

Every telephone pole between the station and the Dollar Plus sported a fluorescent reminder of the upcoming ORV Fest. Not that they were needed. It wasn't as though anyone would drive through St. Sorcha and change their existing weekend plans. The town had her regulars, and they'd all be coming within a fortnight. The colorful signs only reminded McClacky of his deadline.

The kid behind the register, Tyler according to his name badge, straightened but barely looked up from his phone as the cops entered with a chime. No one wanted to pay full price for something in St. Sorcha, and the Dollar Plus was a haven for thrifty shoppers. Nothing down the rows of linoleum was name-brand, and that was precisely how the regulars and renters liked it. Junior Detective Dunn pushed open the chest freezer, dug for a rainbow popsicle from last season, and popped it in his mouth before disappearing around a display of country-style welcome signs.

McClacky approached them, tracing a finger along the cheap, rough wood emblazoned with stars and patriotic colors. He wondered who would buy such a gaudy thing, as half the cottages in town already had one on their front porch beside refurbished rockers. Such a minor detail wasn't in the official reports, but every one of the murder scenes had such a sign out front. Taking note of trivia made him good at his job, but it wasn't like it meant anything.

Dunn returned with a red plastic basket loaded with an example of each department in the Dollar Plus. A bottle of concentrated floor cleaner, completely in Spanish, two individually wrapped rolls of one-ply toilet paper, a large-print crossword puzzle book, a bag of taffy, and a dusty paperback novel. Still sucking on the popsicle, Dunn paid and looked expectantly at McClacky.

"You sure you don't need anything?"

"Signs're on sale," Tyler offered with a nod.

McClacky's eye drifted to the cheap welcome signs and, for the first time in years, thought how Clara might have happily put several just like it on their front stoop. "Quite sure. I do my shopping off duty. Come on, junior detective."

He pulled a cigarette from the pack in his breast pocket and lit it the moment they stepped on the rubber mat outside.

"You know those'll kill you," said Dunn in a tone McClacky was sure the kid intended as helpful or informative. It only made the senior officer want to knock him over the head.

"Welp, something's gotta do it." Leaning against the side of the patrol car, McClacky nodded his chin to the mass-market paperback in the kid's hand. "I didn't know your generation read. Just video games and books on tape."

"Books on tape," Dunn repeated back with a snort. "Wow, no. They still teach reading in public ed. Maybe don't focus on writing cursive and how to balance a checkbook. No, I read plenty."

McClacky grunted, tossing away the remains of his smoke and reaching for another. "Then what've you got there?"

Dunn held out the paperback up for McClacky. "Crimson Secrets: The Bloodline Chronicles," the senior detective read, eyes drifting to meet Dunn's. "Sounds like smut."

Dunn snatched it back before McClacky could turn it over to read the back. He fidgeted with it, fanning a thumb through the pages. "I mean, there's usually some of that, but it isn't why I read them. It's a whole series, *The Bloodline Chronicles*. It follows a police officer that's also a vampire, and he uses his powers to solve crimes, and the cases are all based on real cases."

"That sounds terrible."

Dunn pursed his lips. "I'm just not explaining it well. They're really good books."

"I'm sure." McClacky flicked away his second butt. "We're on the clock. Unless your book can tell us how to catch this killer, we have work to do."

"Yeah, listen to this," said Dunn as he buckled his seatbelt, reading from the back of his novel. "As darkness descends, Damien Darkwood, a seasoned vampire police officer with an insatiable thirst for justice, faces his most formidable case yet. Tasked with unraveling the enigmatic puzzle, Damien must navigate the intricate web of deceit, secrecy, and ancient bloodlines. With his unique abilities and unwavering determination, he must confront both supernatural and human forces that threaten to plunge the town into eternal night. As the clock ticks and the body count rises, Damien races against time to expose the truth and protect his community from an encroaching evil that transcends mere mortals. Will he succeed in solving this haunting mystery, or will he become the next victim in the relentless dance between darkness and light?"

McClacky grunted, silently cursing the captains that kept assigning him to the least senior officers on the force. "That's a lot of words without saying anything."

"Yeah, well." Dunn fanned a finger through the book again. "This is the sixteenth in the series. The author must be doing a good job for a little nothing town like this carry his work."

McClacky bit back the grin that threatened at the edge of his lips.

"But imagine it," Dunn continued. "What if this killer was a vampire? All the victims have had a welcome sign on their front porch."

They pulled up to a red light, details gnawing at the back of McClacky's mind. "You noticed all the victims had a welcome sign out front?"

Dunn nodded with a mouth full of taffy. "Yeah. 'Welcome to our lake house. Hang up your towel and come on in' and the like. I figured you decided it wasn't important since, like, everyone has those up here. That would probably give a Dracula permission to come in and kill you. It would explain all the blood, too."

"A Dracula? Is that what you kids call them these days?"

"Sure." Dunn shrugged. "I never got why vampires make such a mess. I don't throw potato salad all over the room when I'm eating it, so why do they splash blood all over?"

"You know vampires aren't real, right kid? I feel like I need to hear you say it."

"I know." Dunn slid his book back into his plastic bag, looking down at his lap. "I know vampires aren't real."

Vampires weren't real, but neither were half the creatures central in McClacky's biggest cases, according to official records.

Most signs had generic greetings, but all the victims had cheap wood and paint that directly welcomed the visitor into their home.

McClacky cursed, hoping the kid hadn't accidentally cracked the case. Sure, closing the last case before retirement would be great, but not if it meant facing off against a bloodsucking creature of hell.

Eh, he'd gone against worse.

"I'm dropping you back at the station. I have some other errands to run."

Dunn's shoulders slumped. "You sure? I can go with you."

"Yeah, kid. See you in the morning."

Hopefully.

Twenty minutes later, McClacky dug through the shed behind his cottage, sifting through years of unplayed yard games until he found a slice of the elm tree that was once in his front yard. Burned into the rings was the text, "Welcome, come on in! Seamus and Clara McClacky, est 1978." He propped it against the siding beside the front door and stepped into the cabin that should have been his retirement home. Pouring a tall glass of whiskey, he pried up the loose floorboard, removing the polished box below it. The weight of his father's service revolver settled comfortably into his grip, but the special bullets he loaded into the cylinder filled him with dread for the night to come.

***

No amount of unease could stave off the exhaustion that came with keeping his nerves on high alert for hours. McClacky snorted awake as a shadow flitted across the lacey curtain over the the front window. Decades of detective experience kicked in to analyze the image that he only glimpsed for an instant. Man-shaped, tall and thin, long fingers outstretched. The classic image of shadowy Nosferatu slinking up the stairs came to mind. McClacky clutched his father's gun tight, checking that it hadn't come unloaded while he dozed.

A muffled scratching from the front porch. McClacky pulled back the hammer. He clearly remembered locking the door, but the knob jiggled twice, then twisted freely. It swung inward with a creak, casting a blade of moonlight across the worn berber.

McClacky's heart thudded in his ears, so thunderous he barely heard the hissed voice. "If you didn't want to be my meal, perhaps you shouldn't have been quite so cavalier about broadcasting your welcoming invitation."

The clawed shadow stood silhouetted in the open doorway. It took one step forward, crossing into the cabin.

McClacky squeezed his finger.

The creature bellowed its rage as 38-caliber slugs ripped apart its damned soul. It collapsed in a heap after McClacky fired the last. He shook out the casings and reloaded before approaching to kick the mass with his boot. He rolled it over, barely registering the twisted pale flesh and steaming black blood. His eyes could only see the rectangle of plastic on his chest.

Tyler, Dollar Plus.

"Quite the mess you got here, McClacky."

He jumped at the voice behind him, close enough to feel the cold breath on his neck. He wheeled, tripping on the body and losing his gun to flailing arms.

Junior Detective Miles Dunn stepped into the sliver of moonlight; his mouth twisted into a feral grin with unnaturally long canines.

"Why are you..." McClacky looked down at the body, then back to his partner. "Was he even one of them, or just your decoy?" He scanned the floor for his revolver.

Dunn's eyes sparkled with an inner hellfire. He raised McClacky's father's service arm, turning it to dump the special munitions on the floor. "Don't worry, old man. You've solved your last case. I don't know how I'll spin this when I arrive at the scene in the morning, but that's hours away."

"But... I've seen you both in the sun."

Dunn snorted and shrugged. "So?"

"You monster." His fingers slipped around the aerosol can clipped to his belt. Its contents would definitely not be found on the shelves of the Dollar Plus.

"If it comes to name-calling, I think we're done here. It was an honor, McClacky. I'll make sure to keep the scene consistent and get your..." He chuckled wryly. "*Potato salad* all over the place. I told you my books were based on true cases."

"I must be out of practice, two weeks from retirement. I never deduced that I worked beside a celebrity, Damien Darkwood."

Dunn grinned, flashing slender canines in the dark.

McClacky raised the can, bringing it in front of him just as Dunn closed the space between them.

A Polka Break

My first concert was Weird Al Yankovic in… maybe 1995 or '96. *Amish's Paradise* was his current top hit, and he had a costume change for every song. Sounds exhausting. Fast forward to 2023, I just saw him on his "Ill-Advised Vanity Tour," where he played only his originals rather than the parody hits that made him famous. Well, he couldn't *not* do any parodies, so the encore included a medley of them to a smooth jazz beat. It struck me, the number of jumps needed to appreciate that. Genius.

Not that I'd put myself on the level of a brilliant mind such as Weird Al's, but I drew a parallel between his albums and a volume of *Ooo Shiny!* Different genres, different styles, some are parodies, some try to be a little more serious.

Anywho, you're about eight stories in now, assuming you're reading these in order, and you're probably looking back at the cover thinking, "Aren't these supposed to be about holidays?" Well, again, an adult with untreated ADHD wrote this book. The one about the writer summoning a fae took place during Diwali and the intergalactic zoo was inspired by my thoughts in regards to Earth Day. The squonk came from New Year's and the dragons went on their date on Valentine's Day.

This is how my brain works. I hear something that reminds me of something else, to something else, and a few times more. I start my story and get blank stares and blinks from the others in the room, wondering how the hell I got onto such a different topic. No! I promise that was somehow related! So, I have to walk them through my nest of thoughts.

It all makes perfect sense.

Morty and the Dreidel Dragon

This was it. Morty held his kerosene lamp high in one hand, casting shaky light over the deep etching in the stone door. In his other, he raised his tattered diary to compare the symbol to his grandfather's delicate drawing. Not that he needed to. He had every detail of the journal committed to memory after so many years of study.

Yet he couldn't remember where he left his glasses.

"Oh yes." His words echoed down the wide hall behind him as he pulled his glasses down from where they rested on his balding head.

The world came into sharper focus, blasting away any lingering doubts.

Morty wondered how to open the door with no handle, but maybe... He pressed a shoulder against the stone, digging the hard leather of his boot into the floor. Something grumbled deep in the cavern around him, and he quickly hopped back from the door. Or at least he intended to. The stone slid into the ground, and Morty toppled forward, rolled once head over heels, to lie flat on his back, staring up at the ceiling of the hexagonally shaped chamber. His lamp landed a few feet away, reflecting and redoubling its light, slowly raising the ambient luminance, and bringing the room into focus.

Each side of the sharply cut stone sported a door like the one Morty had entered through. The floor sloped down gently to the center, whereupon on top of an uneven pile of what looked like wooden blocks sat the very object of his quest. The Menorah of Miracles glistened silver in the growing light, each of its nine slender candles ending in a delicate wick. At a glance, it didn't look any different from the menorahs seen in every window back home, but as he watched, the shamash lit with a playful flicker.

"This was too easy!" Morty shoved the worn journal into his pocket. It hadn't been easy up to this point, after fleeing his cursed village, leaving his wife and children behind. He trekked a quarter of the way around the world chasing one false lead after another, narrowly dodging death a dozen times until he finally arrived at the door from his grandfather's journal. But all that seemed forgotten when finally faced with victory. Oh, would his grandmother be proud! Only a dozen feet remained between him and breaking the ancient curse.

Three steps forward, something growled deep, vibrating the smooth floor, and Morty's feet slid from under him. He landed hard, whirling back to see the door he'd come through sliding upward. He scrambled to find purchase on the smooth stone, but the door was sealed tight by the time he reached it. The deep, vibrating growl continued. The hairs on Morty's neck tingled as something clattered lethargically behind him. With a hand still on the door, he turned.

A pale blue reptilian hand with three clawed fingers dug through the mountain beside the Menorah of Miracles. Then another on the opposite side. The source of the growl came next, a long, scaled snout and eyes that trailed icy white mist.

A dragon.

Morty groaned. Of course, it wouldn't be so easy in the final moments.

It coiled its long form once around the menorah. Easily ten feet long, it dug the claws of each of its four stout legs into what Morty could now see weren't cubes but dreidels—thousands of them. There was nothing about this in his grandfather's journal, but there was nothing about what lay beyond the runed door.

"Mortimer Schlepperstein," it growled. "I see your heart and your quest."

"That'll save some time," Morty said to himself and cleared his throat. He surveyed the mountain of tops, wondering how he might ascend it without being buried within it. "Oh great, erm, Dreidle Dragon. Could you pass me the Menorah of Miracles?"

The dragon's snorting laughter made Morty's teeth rattle.

"Why are you laughing?"

"I have watched your quest for forty moons, yet you surprise me, Mortimer Schlepperstein. Your directness is...refreshing."

"Well, as you say, it's been over three years since I left home, and I want to get back. The Menorah is right there and—"

"Enough! You will have the Menorah if you prove to me the blood of your noble ancestors flows through you. Answer me three riddles." It raised its front-left arm, extending three clawed digits. "I come in a box, with letters you see. Spinning 'round and 'round, won't you play with me? I have four sides and a letter on each face. Guess quickly now, what am I in this playful chase?"

Morty's eye flickered to the mountain below the dragon as uncertainty crept around him. The answer was too obvious. "A dreidle."

The dragon lowered one claw. "I'm a tasty delight, a treat so grand. Fried in oil, and I'm in high demand. Powdered with sugar or a jelly-filled sweet. Can you name this Hanukkah treat?"

Morty's stomach growled with the very thought. How long had it been since he had more than dry rations on his trek? "A sufganiyah." Morty licked his lips.

Only one claw remained. "I'm a symbol of Hanukkah, shining so bright. Lit up in the windows, a beautiful sight. I have branches and candles, each night I grow. Tell me now, can you guess, what am I in the glow?"

"A menorah."

The dragon closed its fist and slid around the Menorah of Miracles once, then again, gaining speed until I was a pale blue blur. Then, with a soft pop, it was gone. The Menorah tipped forward, tumbling down the stack of dreidels, and Morty rushed forward to catch it before it hit the smooth stone ground. The polished silver felt cold against his fingers and he caught the reflection of his deep, tired eyes in its gleam. Finally, he held what could reverse the curse put against his little home village all those decades ago. He took the shamash with trembling fingers and transferred the light to the other eight candles. He whispered a prayer to the Lord our God, King of the universe, who performed miracles for his ancestors. He asked for another miracle, to restore life and light to his frozen village. To return laughter and joy to a place cursed so long ago.

With a deep WHOOMP that blasted back his simple clothes, he knew his request had been heard. It had been too easy. All that remained would be to return home to his family.

Except... He spun a slow circle. The six stone doors around the room were identical. No matter, if he got through one, they would all eventually lead him home. It wasn't like each was linked to a separate world. That would be silly.

Morty took out his grandfather's journal, preparing to backtrack through the notes, eager to return to his wife and children, hoping they would recognize him after more than three hard years away.

He dropped the journal with a gasp. Blue scales sprouted from the back of his hand. His index and middle fingers stuck together, as did his ring and pinky, merging into a single clawed digit each. The transformation overwhelmed Morty, and he fell forward on four stout legs. Wrapping his slender tail around the Menorah of Miracles, he climbed the pile of dreidels without displacing a single one. Setting the Menorah at the top, Morty curled around it, watching the slender candles slowly burn down.

The dreidels shifted under him, and a man wearing something like his grandfather might have crawled from the mountain. Adjusting his hat, he picked up the journal and turned to Morty. "Thank you for freeing me. I'll leave this somewhere so someone else might come to free you in a generation. Shalom!"

Morty wanted to speak but was too tired. He could only watch the stranger exit through one of the stone doors, leaving him alone.

When the last light went out, Morty exhaled an icy breath, extinguishing the shamash and closing his eyes to sleep, to wait for the next brave soul seeking the power of the Menorah of Miracles.

People Teeth

"**A**ren't they adorable?"

Ted looked up from his phone to the subject of his mother-in-law's cooing tone. Two small carved quartz statues sat on the dining table in front of his husband. At a distance, they looked like cats until Ted reached to pick one up, and the details from the uncanny valley overran his senses; that genetic horror of something so nearly, but not quite, human. What resembled an everyday tabby lying down with her front paw crossed had too many rolls, and was too oddly proportioned. The tilt of her head was unsettling in a way Ted wouldn't be able to describe to his coworkers at the stand-up meeting tomorrow morning.

"Thanks, Ma," said Mika with honesty that Ted almost believed.

"When I saw them on the shelf, I just couldn't leave them there!" Mika's mother continued, oblivious to Ted's poor attempts at hiding his disgust.

"I'm sure you couldn't," said Mika. "We should get going. Corgs has been locked up all evening."

"Oh sure, sure." Mika's mother blustered to shove a stack of plastic containers crammed with leftovers into a grocery bag and saw them to the door.

"You should have gotten that role at the community theatre, love," Ted said as soon as the car doors were shut. "And also... What in gay hell are these abominations?" He held the other up to the lights on the car's dashboard; a cat sitting back on its haunches with a broad smile.

"Ma has very different tastes." Mika backed out of the driveway.

"It has goddamn people teeth, Mika. People teeth."

Mika smirked. "It's a Cheshire cat."

"It's nasty, is what it is. How quickly can we drop them off at the donation place?"

"You know we have to have them out at Thanksgiving next week. Ma will notice."

"We don't even have cats." Ted dropped the little statues into the bag beside the leftover meatloaf.

"No, but she knows you had them growing up."

"Oh, so it's my fault she thought we'd want these?"

"Yes."

Ted huffed and crossed his arms.

Mika gave him a quick glance and said in a sing-song tone, "Love you, babe." He reached to tickle Ted's knee.

"Don't touch me. Love you too."

Ser Corgnealius rushed through their legs the moment Mika opened the side door of the house. "Sorry, dude," he called after the corgi.

Ted set the plastic bag on the kitchen island, and Mika immediately reached in for the two cat statues. "I think these little guys can go right..." He stepped to the sink and set them on the window sill overlooking it. "Here."

"Gross," Ted muttered across the island.

"Be nice. Don't make me remind you about the Avatar sheet set your mom got us a couple of years ago."

"I think you just did." Ted took a deep breath, exhaling it to the ceiling. "It was nice that your mother thought of us, of me, like that. At least my mom drinks when she shops, so she doesn't remember half the crap she gets us."

Mika walked around the island and put his hands on Ted's cheeks with a smile. "I'm going to get ready for bed. Listen for Corgs, and I'll see you in a few."

***

Ted woke with a gasp. He pushed to his elbows with his heart racing while he struggled to focus on slowing his breath. If it was a nightmare, nothing remained of it except a residual panic.

Mika jerked upright beside Ted, clutching his chest and breathing fast and deep.

"Mika! Mika, you're okay. Just a dream. We both had a bad dream."

"Corgs—" Mika ignored Ted and leaned forward to feel the dog lightly snoring between them. His shoulders relaxed in the dim light of the half-moon. Mika laid back, taking Ted's hand in his. "That was terrible. I don't know what it was, but something was happening to Corgs."

"It was just a dream. He's fine." Ted started to say something about having the protection of the Seelie Court and the fae therein, but there was no need to dredge up memories of their summer at three in the morning.

Between them, Ser Corgnealius yipped once and jumped off the bed in what sounded like an ungraceful landing.

"Ser..." Ted tried to sit up, but this body didn't respond, as if that terrifying sleep paralysis struck him while nearly fully awake. Nails clicked on the hardwood down the hall; Ser Corgnealius recovered from his tumble and on his way for a nighttime snack.

"I can't move, Ted."

Mika's hand felt limp in his.

"What—" A suffocating weight pressed the words from Ted. Wind like a gasp from the grave whistled past his ears.

"Who are you to invoke our name?" The voice whispered in his ear. Ted felt the chill breath of the unseen speaker, but could not turn to face it. Mika whimpered beside him. Moonlight from the open curtains gathered on the ceiling directly over the bed and shrouded the rest of the room in pure darkness. It swirled in a slow spiral, forming something like a face with a wide smile and large, pearl-white, people teeth.

The paralysis lifted enough for them to speak, but not enough to move.

"This house is under the protection of the faeries of the Seelie Court," gasped Mika.

A cold breath exhaled a laugh at Ted's neck. "The fae Courts are nothing."

"What are you?" Ted managed.

"I am the end of hope. The seed of despair. The incarnate of nightmare. The—"

"Yeah, all that," said Mika. "Saying this house is under the protection of fae isn't just a name drop. We've been through some shit." He grunted and pushed up his elbows, staring up at the Cheshire grin floating in space above them.

Nails clicked on the hardwood, growing louder.

"Insolence…"

"No," said Ted. "We just don't need all the foreplay. Why are you here?"

Ser Corgnealius climbed his stairs at the foot of the bed and spat something heavy onto the comforter between them. Ted knew his dog well enough to recognize the feeling of him bringing a toy to chew on in bed. A sharp crack echoed across the bedroom and the paralysis lifted.

"What?" the chill voice sounded confused, distant.

Ted sat bolt upright and by the swirling moonlight, recognized the quartz statuette of the cat sitting back on his haunches. The one with people teeth. He reached for it, but the corgi snatched it up with a playful growl. Ser bit down with another loud crack.

"No!" bellowed the grave voice and the image of the grin overhead faltered. "My idol! How does that beast possess my idol?"

"My ma found it at the thrift store," said Mika. He reached to take the statue from the corgi, who growled and flopped his head side to side. The quartz cracked again and moonlight spun away from the Cheshire grin, returning to the floor and far wall where it should be.

"The other one," Mika said, but Ted already had his bare feet on the floor, racing to the kitchen in just his boxers. The lounging cat statue sat where Mika had placed it and Ted spared only the barest wonder as to how the stumpy legged corgi managed to get the other one from the window sill. He stopped wondering about the minor miracles of his dog months ago.

Lounging cat in hand, he almost tripped over Ser Corgnealius as he turned.

"What's this, boy? What's this?"

Ser's tongue lolled as his head whipped back and forth, excited for what his dad held.

"What's this?"

Ser yipped and jumped up on his hind legs, pawing at Ted's hand.

Ted sank to a squat, lowering the statue and Ser Corgnealius bit down on it with a loud crack, followed by an ethereal moan of the eldritch horror trapped within as it lost its connection to the mortal realm. He dropped the statue and let the dog chew on it. Ted dropped to his seat and leaned against the cabinets.

Mika sat beside him, holding the grinning cat statue. Ted expected to see it mangled with deep dog bites, but the quartz looked as smooth as when he picked it up from his mother-in-law's dining table.

"Okay, you win." Mika leaned his head on Ted's shoulder. "This is far worse than the Avatar sheets. But..."

"Don't say it."

"We still have to put these out at Thanksgiving."

Egg Hunt

Regen stood surrounded by screaming children. Shrill cries of glee made her wince as another rushed by. She wore the itchy pastel dress and gleaming shoes her mothers bought her specifically for this event, but at ten, she was already far beyond the infantile excitement of an egg hunt. Who cared that the president of the United States was right over there, smiling and clapping for the children? She certainly did not.

Another piercing cry shattered the air as a toddler wobbled by, spilling plastic eggs from his basket. Regen looked down at her own, half empty. With a sigh, she picked up the child's discarded chocolate containers and dropped it in with her others, knowing Mama would be upset if she didn't have at least a few more. There had hardly been any other topic at dinner since receiving notice they had won a ticket in the lottery. Mama would expect a full basket and an efficient time of enjoyment.

Regen spotted a bright red egg at the edge of a bush and moved to claim it. When she knelt, she saw another further into the hedge. Branches tugged at her hair and dress while her polished shoes sank into the soft dirt, but it wasn't just one more egg, but a half dozen. Arranged in something akin to a bird's nest, the crimson eggs looked scaly in the dim light. Regen picked up one the size of her fist, surprised by the weight and how the surface felt like the leather couch from the living room. She dropped one into her basket, remembering Mum's words, only to take one at a time and save them for the other children.

The bumbling child with an overflowing basket replayed in Regen's mind.

Those other kids had plenty.

She took every egg, wondering what special prize she might receive for finding the special clutch—probably a giant bunny candy or something similarly asinine. Children were simple to impress with chocolate. Regen turned to exit the hedge but paused before stepping back into the lawn. The heavy eggs glistened in the dappled sunlight. These were too nice to turn over for a hollow chocolate lagomorph. She shuffled them to the bottom, covering them with a layer of bright plastic shells.

Her concerns were unfounded, as no one paid attention to her basket's contents. The president said a little something, and men in dark suits ushered everyone quickly out to give them time to reset for the eleven o'clock hunt.

Mama drove, and Mum twisted in her seat to smile back at Regan. "Looks like you found a lot of eggs! Did you have fun, my tiny?"

Regan considered the heavy stone eggs with the leathery touch. She would keep that her secret, at least for now, though she couldn't quantify why, even to herself. Taking a single sky-blue egg from the top, she smiled and handed it forward. Mum cracked it with a nail to dump the two silver-foil-wrapped treasures into her palm.

"So sweet of you! I'm glad you had a good time today." She turned forward to open the candy.

Did she have fun? Regen couldn't decide. The solid weight on her lap made her think she did.

Upon arriving home, Regan arranged the stone eggs in a pile of coats at the back of her closet. They were her secret, her thing she could keep from the world.

Until a week later, when she woke to find they were nothing but shattered remains and a slimy trail leading to the open window. In another few days, she waited outside the kitchen while her mothers discussed in hushed tones, worrying over the cases of "petrification" showing up at the hospitals. Regan had to look up the word, which led her to articles about its use in recent popular fiction. Returning to her closet, she held the shell remains against the artist's rendering of a basilisk egg—a near-perfect match.

* * *

What happens next? Did she save the president by removing basilisk eggs from the White House lawn or doom the world by taking them from the secure perimeter?

This story started with the thought of "a kid finds something weird in their basket after an Easter egg hunt." I did WAY too much research into the White House Easter Egg Roll procedure. It was originally from one of the mom's point of view, and after 200 words, the kid was just being woken up. It is interesting how a story can evolve quickly, even as short as this.

The Chicken

I bake naked in the sun but would never complain, for this is my role. I wind through the countryside, carving the critical path. I am relied on by thousands; it has always been my noble duty in this world.

What's this now? Some reluctant traveler wishes to pass my girth rather than my length. What does this mean? Treating me as an entity which divides the world rather than uniting its farthest reaches. Do I divide? Is my existence a lie? Do I render the world in twain?

Seeds. Seeds there. The ground is hot. Hurts my feet. Run faster. Flap my wings. Worthless. Are those seeds? Flap. Flap.

***

Seriously? Answering "Why did the chicken cross the road" by anthropomorphizing the road?

Healers

Celeste von Dewer Bronman paused with a hand flat on the door, steeling the nerve and energy to push it open. She considered fleeing for the millionth time, to return to her flat above the Korean BBQ and her guinea pigs, but the twinge in her back made the decision for her. Within, the other patients sat in cheap plastic chairs, all looking as miserable as she felt with faces twisted in pain.

"Jon," called the nurse, and a withered old man rose, supporting himself with a stout cane.

Celeste von Dewer Bronman signed in at the counter, thinking for the thousandth time to add another bit to her name, or change the spelling, but the doctor would find out. They would always find out. And the law was clear. If they couldn't take one, they would take them all.

She sat in the space vacated by Jon as another nurse appeared at the door. "L," she said, and an old woman was helped to rise by what might be her grandchildren.

Celeste von Dewer Bronman averted her gaze for a moment, unwilling to watch the old woman go to her end, but felt a twang of guilt. She raised her eyes to watch her pass the nurse.

Farewell, L.

***

This was an odd little one. The prompt was something to the effect of, "The doctors don't take money. Instead, they take…" So of course they take a slice of what some people argue is the only thing is truly yours.

Resolution

No more drinking.

No more smoking.

Eat more vegetables.

Exercise.

Save money.

Talk to Dad.

I was doing great with my list, even beating out the mid-January dropoffs at the rec center. Heck, it was almost March before I woke up to unexpected snow, causing my first missed day at the gym, which lead to two, then four... But I got back into it within another week. It's shocking how quickly you lose your gains with the briefest pause.

Cutting out the weekly visits to Ashes to Dust meant no more cigars and no more Scotch, which also checked off the saving money item. Choking down a salad twice a week from the bistro in the lobby at work had been a chore, but now I didn't even think about it. The bistro was called "Lettuce Go" and had an off-brand, copyright side-stepping Mario and Nintendo theme. I thought it was the most bizarre thing until I finally made the connection and felt stupid for taking me so long. I never told anyone, well, before now, that I didn't get it immediately. I suspect I'm not alone in that boat. They hired all of the most weirdly hot people. I swear they were all struggling, dreamful Los Angeles actors... except this is Stillwater, Minnesota. Never heard of it? Don't worry about it. Go Ponies!

That just left one item. When did I last talk to my father? That's a rhetorical question; I knew exactly when. I knew the date and the time. What the wind chill was and the night's snow forecast. What the Powerball estimate was and the mileage on my Chevy. It's odd how a moment can become frozen, perfectly preserved in a person's mind. For my parents, it was where they were when they heard JFK was assassinated. For me, it was watching live TV as a plane hit the south tower.

And leaving Dad's house that night.

It felt like watching some over-acted movie starring actors that were famous fifteen years prior, desperate to revitalize their careers. We fought over the most recent of my relationships. I was, of course, for it, and Dad was vehemently against. He was right, of course, something I see with obvious clarity seven years later. I stormed out, screaming every nasty thing that came to mind, him screaming just as loud, neither of us hearing the other, all while the neighbors watched through the slats of their blinds.

When three days passed, and he hadn't texted to apologize or offer some olive branch, and his Facebook was still clear of vague booking passive aggressiveness three days after that, I declared him the winner. I drove to his house and... Yeah...

"Hey, Dad." I tugged my collar a little higher against the sudden bite of wind. Thunder rumbled, threatening to bathe the park any moment. "I, uh, I got my associate's degree last spring. I know you've been on me about that. I want to keep going, but I'm trying to get work to pay for it. Maddisyn and I broke up pretty soon after we last spoke, I... I know you just always wanted the best for me, and I'm sorry I couldn't see it. I want you to know I'm doing okay now, and that's because of you. Thank you."

I turned to leave but knew there was one more thing he wanted to say. I beat him to it. "I love you, Dad."

I rushed back to my car before he could respond.

* * *

This story was going to have a necromancer, dark magic, ghosts. It's under 600 words and sometime in the hour it took me to write the first draft, I changed it, steering from the fantasy element and setting it in our world. It's not fun and shouldn't make anyone laugh. While you don't want harsh words to be the last exchanged with a loved one, you shouldn't suffer abuse from anyone. Was dad being abusive to our unnamed protagonist? We don't know enough to make a judgment.

I'm no psychologist, but there is value in having those one-sided conversations with someone you've lost. Sometimes just speaking to the void can make you feel heard.

Leohck o' de Green

E oan Ó Bradáin pressed deeper into the stinking heap of trash, hoping the black plastic would obscure the bright green of his top hat and vest. They were coming, streaming past the dark alley with strings of beads about their necks and foam hats that were an oversized mockery of his own. "Kiss Me, I'm Irish!" commanded their pins and discount t-shirts. Eoan huddled tighter, clasping his quavering hands over his mouth to hold back the whimper as the last few stumbled by, arm in arm, singing an off-key tune.

Of all the days to visit Earth, he had to pick this one.

Eoan crept to the corner, peeking out as the last notes of a jaunty tune faded into the growing dark. He looked both ways before sprinting to the garden across the street, diving into the low hedges. Digging through the tight branches, the world suddenly opened around him as he entered the Whimsigrove Market. Faeries seated on huge mushrooms plucked at string instruments without attempting any tune. In contrast, the brownies tried all the tunes at once on their flutes. Scents of a dozen frying meats and tubers hit him from the stalls operated by other leprechauns. He breathed it deeply, but had to jump back as a group of young pookas ran by, still unsure of their shapeshifting powers and currently half formed into different Earth forest creatures.

An ancient man, naked except for the leather sachet strung across his shoulder, shuffled toward him. His liver spotted skin hung loose, and most might confuse him for a human if they didn't look too closely at his eyes.

"Good evenin', Tom," said Eoan. He looked up at the hunched man towering over him, avoiding those eyes.

"Can you believe they're out of nixie again?" Tom huffed, his voice rough and cracked. "I spend a week's worth of magic to get there, and they don't have the one thing I want."

Tom limped off.

"Hey, Eoan," droned a translucent woman in wildly flapping robes.

"'ello and good evenin', Blinne."

"Here for some shopping? Already out of brandywine?"

"Ahh, you know 'ow Coileán and I love our brandywine. Nothin's better dan 'ow de Ó Sés make it."

"I wouldn't know."

"Well, you are a banshee."

"Want to know how you die?"

"No, dank you as always, Blinne."

"Are you sure? It's really good."

Eoan stood on his tiptoes, surveying the tents and stands. "'ave you seen the Ó Sés? I thought dey always 'ad their stall set up on de weekends."

Blinne's sigh was like a breeze scratching against grave moss. "No, but don't worry. I know how they die, and it's not their time yet. Do you want to know how they go? It's messy."

Eoan asked around, but no one had seen the brothers all week. Despite the dangers of their kind even visiting Earth, the Ó Sé brothers worked their distillery full time here, just up the road. Eoan couldn't return home empty-handed, so his next stop was clear.

But...

He thought of the revelers with their tunes as haphazard as the faeries' plucking. More of his brothers than he cared to count were captured by the humans here. Most were killed when they learned his kind didn't all have access to pots of gold. They couldn't even use magic in most places. Why the Whimsigrove Market would set up residence in such a nasty world was still a mystery to him, but it was a convenient crossroads between so many others.

"I can go with you," said Blinne.

As much as he cringed at the thought of a morose banshee's accompaniment, traveling up the road alone was too terrifying.

"Yes, if you don't mind, dank you."

He bought a meat stick on the way from the Whimsigrove Market, glancing back once more at the laughing children and carefree fae before steeling himself for the dread of the human world.

Eoan kept near the hedge's edge, peering for more drunk humans. A dozen loitered, staggering in place, outside The Hidden Harp pub. The Ó Sés distillery was below that. Just two stone throws away, but the presence of humans made it seem like a week's journey at sea.

"You would want to hurry," said Blinne, her moan echoing to the alley across the street.

"What is dat?"

"I thought you didn't want to know?"

Eoan shrank into the hedge as a human on a bicycle passed. "What are you talkin' about?"

The violent, unfelt wind tugging at the banshee's clothes lessened. "You never want to know how people die."

"Are you sayin' de brothers'll die soon?"

Blinne's gale picked up, and she nodded.

Eoan's heart leaped to his throat. "What? 'ow?"

"You want to know?"

He waved her down. "Are dey in de pub?"

"Yes."

Eoan marked a path along the low stone wall bordering the road, noting the dark points between street lights, mapping a route to safely reach the bare bulb lights on the pub's patio. He could get there. The group in front of the pub was breaking apart, some wandering away, some returning inside with a blast of raucous music as they opened the door.

He couldn't access his magic outside of Whimsigrove Market and a few other pockets on Earth. Certainly not down at that pub. What could he do to save them? He had to try.

With a steeling breath, he took one step forward.

The banshee at his side gasped.

"What?" Eoan asked.

"Oh, nothing. Things changed."

"What changed? Are de brothers still in trouble?"

"In trouble, yes, but *they* don't die now."

"I don't like 'ow you stressed dat word."

"You said you don't want to know about your death," said Blinne. "You always get quiet when I try to tell you about it."

"So it's me? I'm goin' to die now?"

Blinne said nothing at first, just stared back at Eoan. "No, it's the brothers again."

"Make up your mind, Blinne!"

"This is amusing, my friend. If you go, you die. If you don't, the Ó Sé brothers die. The outcome continues to shift based on your indecision."

"Can't I do anythin' to save dem while keepin' myself safe?"

"You could have, if you hadn't hesitated after stepping from the bushes."

"I'm too late?"

"No, you don't die if you leave right... now."

"What?"

"Too late."

"Blasted banshee!" Eoan rushed along the stone wall, keeping to the shadows as best he could, knowing if any of the humans saw him, it would mean his torture and death. Blinne kept at his side in full, gently-glowing view. Humans couldn't see her. At least not the normal ones that would be out drinking this night.

He dove into the pile of rubbish out back just as another wave of music heralded the front door swinging open. Eoan crawled to a narrow window, using his jacket's cuff to scrub away decades of grim. There, in The Hidden Harp's dim basement, Liam Ó Sé pulled a long ladle from a bubbling vat while Conner sat at a table measuring dry goods.

"Dey don't look like dey're in any danger. Just workin' away."

Blinne drummed the tips of her fingers together.

A door burst open in the room below, making Conner jump and spill the herbs he held. A red-cheeked human stood there, framed by the light from the stairway behind him. Eoan recognized the bar's owner, as any good leprechaun would. It was rare to find a human that was kind to his people.

"Dang it, Hank," Conner grumbled. "What's with barging in?"

"Hide!" the human gasped.

The brother snapped into motion, diving under their tables as four more humans decked out in beads and green buttons pushed past Hank. One had hair and a beard as bright red as Eoan's, two were a sickly bright green, and the third wore a ridiculous hat.

"There you are, Hank," Red slurred. "We knew you kept the good stuff down here."

"Wussat?" said Hat, leaning heavily against Green One. "Smells {hic} like fruit wine down here."

"Looks like a moonshine rig," said Green Two. "You've been holding out on us, Hank!"

"Is it still me dat dies?" Eoan asked Blinne.

The banshee nodded.

"'ow?"

"The one in the hat tosses you to the one on the left. He misses, and you fall against the boiling vat there. It's horrific." She grinned.

"Throw me? I'm almost dirty inches tall. Why would dey throw me?"

"They're quite drunk."

"I see dat. De brothers look safe. Why would I go in dere?"

"Wussis now?" said Green Two, dropping to their hands and knees beside where Conner had been. The human reached under, flailing an arm.

"Nevermind," said Blinne. "It's just Conner now. It's almost identical, what with being boiled alive. How uninspired."

"No!" Eoan banged on the window. "Stinkin 'umans, leave 'im alone!"

Four sets of drunk eyes, and one of a frazzled barkeep, focused on him through the window.

"Hank!" yelled Hat. "You got freaking leprechauns!"

They rushed through the basement still toward him.

"You again," said Blinne. "Long story short, one of them is holding you, demanding your pot of gold, when you're both hit by a laurey out front. It's quick and mostly painless, which I hear is preferred."

Eoan ran to the edge of the pub's patio just as the cellar door burst open. Red popped their head out, shouting in his direction. "There is it! It's a real, freaking leprechaun!"

"Get his gold!" yelled another.

"And his lucky charms!" yelled a third.

Eoan bolted down the street, knowing he couldn't outrun the humans in a fair race. His only hope was for them to be too inebriated to run straight.

Blinne matched his pace, floating backwards. "Now the one in the hat keeps you chained in his basement until you starve when he's maimed in a snowboarding accident in the Rockies."

He saw it, the hedge leading to the Whimsigrove Market. He could use magic to defend himself there. The magic of the market did weird things to the non-fae, though. Eoan dove for it.

Someone caught his boot.

"I got him!" yelled Hat.

Eoan kicked at the fingers gripping his left boot, grinding his heel into the thumb.

"Ah! Freaking bastard leprechaun!" Hat screeched and released him.

Eoan scrambled backward through the bushes until the comforting jumble of stings and flutes assaulted his ears. He couldn't do more than suck in quick gulps of air, knowing those four would burst through in a second.

Blinne floated by him. "Now you're old on the swing by your mushroom orchards, just hours before Coileán."

Eoan jumped to his feet and away as the bush rustled. Four sprites, each only a few inches tall, stepped out. One was bright red, two a sickly bright green, and the fourth had what looked like a growth on its head. They exclaimed in a high pitch trill that Eoan couldn't understand, obviously shocked by their transformation.

"Hey Eoan, welcome back," said Tom beside him. "You found nixies!" Before he could say anything, and with a motion too fast for Eoan to see, Tom had one of the "nixies" in his mouth. He chewed noisily while the other three squealed in his fist. He dropped them into the sachel at this hip. "Say hello to Coileán for me."

Blinne settled beside Eoan as he watched the old man shamble back to the market, a little pep to his step.

"That was fun," she said.

"Fun? I almost died!"

"But I finally got you to let me tell you how it happens. You two look so happy, totally in love."

"Wait... Were de brothers ever in danger? Did you make de whole din' up?"

She grinned, making Eoan involuntarily cringe. "It was fun. Ta, Eoan." She drifted in the direction Tom had gone.

"Blasted banshee."

The Old Email

As I read the email, I shook my head, and my mouth hung open with the growing ridiculousness.

"Do you have flying cars? Have you run out of oil? Is there peace in the Middle East?"

I sat back to rub my face before hitting reply. My job required I reply to every email and message. I noted the sender's email address.

"At-AOL.com?" I laughed to myself. "Okay, Mr. Rural Utah. 1999 called."

I answered no, no, no, added a block of form text thanking them for their communication, and hit send. Only then did I notice the sender's name, Morgan Fieldmont, was one I saw often. As the company's founder, her oil painting hung in the lobby far below me right now. Clearly a spoof. People have too much free time.

I continued the drudgery of replying to questions other tech support agents labeled "unrelated to business." Two hours later, another email from Morgan hit the top of my inbox.

"What's your favorite number? What time is it when you are?"

"When? Not where? Weirdo." I grumbled and replied, reminding myself they paid me hourly. I didn't have to care about the inane questions I fielded all day. Just reply and move on. I said my favorite number is forty-three because it's one more than the answer to life, the universe, and everything. I added the time, form text, and hit send.

It was almost 4:30, the end of my shift, when MF hit my inbox a third time.

"What stocks had the biggest growth in early 2000?"

"Let me Google that for you!" I opened another browser tab and was surprised I hadn't heard of most of the top 10. After pasting the results into the email, along with the form text, I hit send, locked my laptop, and gathered up my coffee mug and day bag.

The elevator from the sixty-third floor was as empty as normal, thanks to my flex schedule. As I rode, the last email stuck in my mind. Wasn't this billion-dollar company famously founded with gains from Mrs. Fieldmont's clever stock maneuvering just after the Y2K crisis? I was near the doors of the gleaming lobby when someone called out my name.

"Ms. Presson," the man in a dark suit repeated as he approached and offered a manila envelope. "Your services are no longer required, but Mrs. Fieldmont offers this as a parting gift."

I stared at the man as he returned to the elevator, then down at the large envelope in my hand, turning it over to see my name stenciled across the front. Pulling back the brass brads, I peeked in and pulled out the two pieces of paper. One was again addressed to me on official corporate letterhead. I'd normally read the letter first but noticed the other piece of paper was a cashier's check, also with my name.

For the amount of forty-three million dollars.

I staggered back to a chair, my arms heavy and numb, staring at the check with disbelief.

The letter must have contained some "gotcha" about what I'd have to do before cashing the thing, not that there was much I wouldn't do for it. But no. I scanned it, a brief handwritten note thanking me for my prompt and helpful emails, signed by Morgan Fieldmont herself. She finished it with a "P.S. Douglas Adams is a treasure!"

Walpurgisnacht

The phone rang in the middle of the night, jolting me out of a deep sleep. I slapped for it on my nightstand, terrified it would wake the others in my bed. I caught a glimpse of my dad's grinning selfie on the screen as I fumbled it to clatter on the hard floor and under the bed. Straining, I barely reached a finger to swipe him to voicemail. That would only worry him, and he'd call again.

One of the creatures stirred beside me, and I froze. It shuffled and turned over, going still as the dead. I used two fingers to carefully lift the skeletal arm across my chest, scooting across the sheets to the edge. Twenty years of sleeping with my cats and dogs gave me plenty of experience getting out of bed without disturbing the others. I never would have guessed it would apply to this.

I put a foot on the cold floor just as my phone blared again. I swiped it off faster this time, but the inhabitants of the bed stirred. Rising in the beam of moonlight cast through the old dust of their ancient crypt, one stood, outlining a frightening silhouette of unnaturally long fingers ending in deadly claws.

"Sorry, I just need to wee," I cooed, but another rose beside it. Then a third.

Dad called a third time, his selfie casting light across the sunken forms of the creatures from the deepest nightmares. I glanced at my duster hung by the door, wondering if I could get to the contents of its inner pockets before they could be on me.

I thought my dad was always spouting random advice, but I heard his words echo now. "Kill vampires, don't sleep with them."

Captain Squeaks

"Yarr, ye forgot the cover letter on yer report."

"Sorry, Jerry. Sarah already reminded me."

"That be okay, but don't be forgotten it next time."

Todd's eye roll only fueled my grin as I turned away, empty mug in hand. On the way to the break room, I nodded, tipping my hat to the coworkers as I passed them. "Jolly mornin', Dale. Ahoy, Tiffany." They glared back at me, eyes all trailing the long feathers tucked into my hat. Grabbing the pot of coffee, I poured, turning to Stephan sitting alone, eating a breakfast bar and reading from a magazine. "Tis a good brew today."

"Jerry," said a mousy voice from the door. I glanced over to see the intern - I could never remember the interns' names - poking his head in. "Mister Sunwells wants to see you in his office."

"Yarr, I'll be on my way in a bit."

"He wants to see you now," said the kid with an odd sense of finality in his tone.

I frowned. "Yeah, sure. Tell him I'll be right there."

The walk to the floor supervisor's office felt decidedly colder than the jaunt to the break room. I felt like everyone now stared at my hat with anger and jealousy rather than the clear joy they exuded before.

Mister Sunwells was younger than my son and grossly overqualified for his position, a fact he often reminded us of. He didn't glance up from his desk when I knocked at the open door; he just waved at the empty seat. I sat, the leather hat feeling a bit heavier.

He kept reading through one sheet, making notes on another.

I cleared my throat.

He kept reading and scratching notes.

I rolled my coffee mug between my hands, counting out the seconds until I should say something.

I hit twenty-nine and took a deeper inhale.

"Mister Dagortol." Mister Sunwells looked up, pushing the wire-rimmed glasses up his nose with his middle finger, looking like every character in all the animes my grandson loves. His eyes flicked to my hat. "Take that thing off your head."

I grinned wide, preparing a speech about what a festive celebration today should be, but his withering glare dissolved it to an indistinct mumble as I wadded the four-hundred dollar hat in my hands, then set it on the chair beside mine.

"I've no doubt you've heard rumors of budget cuts," said Mister Sunwells, leaning back in his leather executive chair, twirling the Mont Blanc in his fingers like my niece with a drumstick. I wondered if her band would play again soon. They were a bit loud, but the crowd had such a great time. Oops, Mister Sunwells was still talking.

"...by end of day. You will be granted two months severance after signing the paperwork and NDA with HR."

I blinked, taking a moment to process the last bit and stitch it with the rest. "You're firing me?"

"You'll find the severance package to be more than gracious."

"But... I've been with Vatican Harbor Jewels from the beginning. I was on the boat that returned the treasure used to found this company."

"And we thank you for your service." He gestured to the door.

I stood, stunned, and turned to the door.

Mister Sunwells cleared his throat.

"Take that lice-ridden thing with you." He pointed at my hat.

Packing up my desk was easy. There were no personal pictures or trinkets, just a lot of stress balls shaped like barrels, buttons, mugs, and water bottles with the stenciled ship company logo. What irony, to be fired on National Talk-Like-A-Pirate-Day from a company started by the capital from long-lost pirate booty.

I glanced to ensure no one was looking my way before slipping my fingers under my keyboard tray, feeling for the folded paper taped underneath. Pulling it free, I grinned at the weight of what was folded within. I dropped that into my pocket.

All eyes were downcast on my way to the elevator. I'd worked here longer than most of my coworkers had been alive, so naturally, they were devastated to see me go. Maybe this was fine. Maybe it was time to retire. I didn't need the money; work was more of an excuse to leave the apartment so my gerbils would be happy to see me when I came home.

The doors opened with a ding, and four men dressed as stereotypical Caribbean pirates stepped out in a rush. I sidestepped, tipping my hat to the quality of their costumes. Were they a team from Legal coming down for a meeting? How great.

"Yar! Keep yer hands where we can see 'em!" one shouted, and someone else screamed.

Maybe not from Legal.

One of the pirates, which I assumed was the captain by the gems woven into his long beard and a feather in his hat that sparked a bit of jealousy, climbed up on Sarah's desk. He kicked her tray of succulents and waved his very large, very period-appropriate pistol.

Definitely not from Legal.

"We've come fer the loot ye pilfered from us," said the one on the desk. All my former co-workers huddled beside their chairs, hands clasped over their hands. Mister Sunwells' office door closed with a quiet click.

Pilfered? The weight in my pocket seemed a little weightier. I slowly reached a finger in, pushing away the paper to feel the uneven edges of the thin coin. The Vatican Harbor Corporation sold off the last doubloon years ago. Even the one on display in the lobby was a replica.

At least the last according to their official records.

"I can smell it," said the captain, inhaling deeply through blocked sinuses.

The elevator door remained open, yet to be beckoned to another floor. I thought of my gerbils, but a pirate had the intern by his lapel. The kid looked ready to wee himself. As much as I wanted to continue out of the office to enjoy the afternoon stroll back to my flat, I couldn't help but feel invested in the situation.

"Ye 'ave to the count o' ten, but I'll warn ye, old Mad Eyes 'ere will skip the numbers 'e doesn't know." The captain shouted, waving at a pirate sporting an eyepatch.

"One... Two... uh..." Mad Eyes struggled.

I took a step away from the elevator, clearing my throat. "Hello there. I may have what you're looking for." Setting down my box of personal items, I fished the coin from my pocket, holding it high.

The captain jumped down and rushed toward me. His wild eyes moved over my hat with its inferior feather, and he grinned, exposing teeth in desperate need of a dental plan. "Jolly work, brother! Since ye found it, ye can decide the fate of these thieves."

"Um..." I looked past the captain to my former co-workers, unsure of what options there were.

"Shall I scuttle 'em?" Mad Eyes offered.

"Oh no!" I waved my hands wildly. "Not that. Leave them be. They were just keeping the doubloon safe here."

Mad Eyes' shoulders drooped, and he kicked at the carpet.

"Come, matey! Let's get back t' the ship." The captain clapped me on the shoulder, pushing me toward the awaiting elevator.

I'd be lying if I said that wasn't the strangest elevator ride of my life, with four seventeenth-century pirates pressed around me. I still had time to smile, thinking I'd avoid the exit interview with HR. It wasn't until the door opened to the expansive windows overlooking the city that I realized we'd been going up. The high-level officers were all empty - likely everyone whose title started with a 'C' was out playing golf today.

Sometimes we see something so impossible to believe that we accept it. If pirates attack my office on the 19th of September, why shouldn't they have arrived in a three-masted Man o' War?

And there it was, moored to the corner office balcony, floating sixty-three floors over the streets of Vatican Harbor. I kept my gaze forward as I crossed the narrow gangplank, where two dozen more pirates cheered our arrival. The captain grabbed my wrist, raising my hand to show the coin I still held. The cheers doubled.

They surrounded me, slapping me on the back, gapped and rotted smiles grinning with genuine joy. I smiled back. I couldn't help but to. Their happiness was real, infectious, and I realized my co-workers' smirks were always forced.

"This scallywag has saved us!" bellowed the captain. "Hail Brother..." He paused, looking at me with brows raised.

"Jerry. Jerry Dagortol."

"Yar, this a good name fer ye."

A tankard of ale was pressed into my hand. I'd made it my practice not to drink before four in the afternoon, but apparently, I was a member of a seventeenth-century Caribbean pirate crew on an airship. My old rules went out the window.

Thinking of windows, I looked past my raucous crewmates and saw only blue, open ocean. Any hint of the iconic Vatican Harbor skyline was gone.

"Captain," I called. "Can the ship take on four more... shall I call them crewmates?"

"Yar, fer ye, Brother Jerry, whatever ye be wantin'."

"Can we stop by my place for my gerbils?"

GNORMAN

"We are Gnorman. We are one."

The tyrannosaurus reared back, bellowing its rage as the Gnormans clung desperately to its massive scales, their tiny forms barely visible against the ferocious beast. With tooth and claw, the dinosaur thrashed, but the Gnormans remained steadfast, their collective voices resounding in unison.

"We are Gnorman. We are one," they chanted, undeterred even as the dinosaur snapped at them, spitting out a bright green, steepled hat. Emerging from the hedges, more Gnormans appeared in vibrant red or blue jackets, their tall hats reaching down to their bulbous noses, and white beards flowing to their belts. The tyrannosaurus spun, lashing out its tail, leaving only gleaming black boots in its wake as it struck the Gnormans.

"We are Gnorman." Two more fell to the crushing jaws of the beast, their diminutive bodies no match for its colossal teeth. "We are one." Another was flattened beneath its stomping foot.

The tyrannosaurus fought with relentless determination, refusing to retreat or surrender. But against a force without fear, an army united in unwavering solidarity, resistance was futile.

They were Gnorman. They were one.

***

Abby paused, her laughter bubbling up at the sight of a lawn ornament near the gate. She nudged Liz with her elbow, pointing with a mischievous grin. "Look at that. Poor gnomes."

The Missed Date

Simon looked at his smart watch for the sixteenth time. No messages. He pulled out his phone to ensure the two were still connected and opened the messaging app. No messages. He opened the thread with Tim, confirmed the date, time, and location, checked the date and time were definitely correct, and this was the only sushi bar in their backwater beach town. Simon was in the right place at the right time, so where the hell was Tim?

He continued scrolling on his phone. Every other social media account showed Tim hadn't been active any sooner than six hours ago.

"He better be dead," Simon grumbled. "I shouldn't say that. I don't mean that."

The waiter cycled by, glared at Simon's water, and asked again if he was ready to order. Simon waved him off with a half-hearted smile and Googled the county morgue's website.

The door slammed open with an angry jingle of the bell. Other patrons gasped, pulling Simon's attention to Tim rushing at him; shirt ripped and spattered with what looked like blood.

He rushed to Simon's table, his red-rimmed eyes wide. "We have to go. Now." He snatched Simon's hand and pulled him from his seat with surprising force. "The gerbils. My god, the gerbils."

Post-Yammering

Yeah... I promised the holiday edition, and that didn't last, now did it? I feel like staying on target wouldn't be staying on brand. Not that the second book in a series constitutes "a brand." But, if you're planning a strawberry festival, not all the decorations have to be strictly strawberries, right? I'm sure that example is somehow relevant.

What was I talking about...?

Ooo Shiny! is my little celebration of how my brain works. I'm either hyperfocused or not at all, with little in between. I feel like it's gotten worse since turning forty. Yet, it is possible to get something accomplished. As of typing this sentence, I've written six novels, hold down a good job as a programmer, and will be testing soon to be a fourth-degree black belt. I've talked with so many amazing people at book shows that share my attributes, and always encourage them to strive for their goals.

As much as I want to focus on my fantasy novels, these little stories bubble around in my brain. They're just fun. Fun to write, fun to explore different narration and writing styles, and fun to try different genres. They're easy for a reader that may not have the time or mental energy for a 300-page novel.

If you've enjoyed a single story here, or even if you didn't, check out my other works.

About the Author

Author Jamie M. Samland is a mathematician by training, a web developer by profession, and a martial artist and writer by passion. Math nerd, cat dad, gamer. He always loved to write, but what started in force during the 2020 lockdown has become a driving passion.

Jamie lives in Michigan with his husband and their furbabies.

As a self-published author, he relies on awesome people like you to grow, so please consider leaving a review on Good Reads and your point of purchase. Find him on TikTok, Facebook, Instagram, or at www.jamiemsamlan d.com.

Also By

Books by Jamie M. Samland:

Realms of Terswood (2020)
Trials of Throk'tar (2021)
Necromancer of Urbus (2022)
Seeds of Farsil (2022)
Ooo Shiny! Volume 1 (2022)
Arcanym (2023)
The Invisible Castle (2023)
Ooo Shiny! Volume 2, Holiday Edition 1 (2023)